This is an Alyson Wonderland book from
Alyson Publications, 40 Plympton St., Boston, Mass. 02118.
Distributed in England by GMP Publishers.

First edition, first printing: November 1990.

ISBN 1-55583-178-8
LC #90-45593

Typeset in the United States of America.
Printed in Hong Kong by Paper Communication.

Daddy's
Roommate

by Michael Willhoite

To my Dad

My Mommy and Daddy got a divorce last year.

Now there's somebody new at Daddy's house.

Daddy and his roommate Frank live together,

Work together,

Eat together,

Sleep together,

Shave together,

And sometimes even fight together,

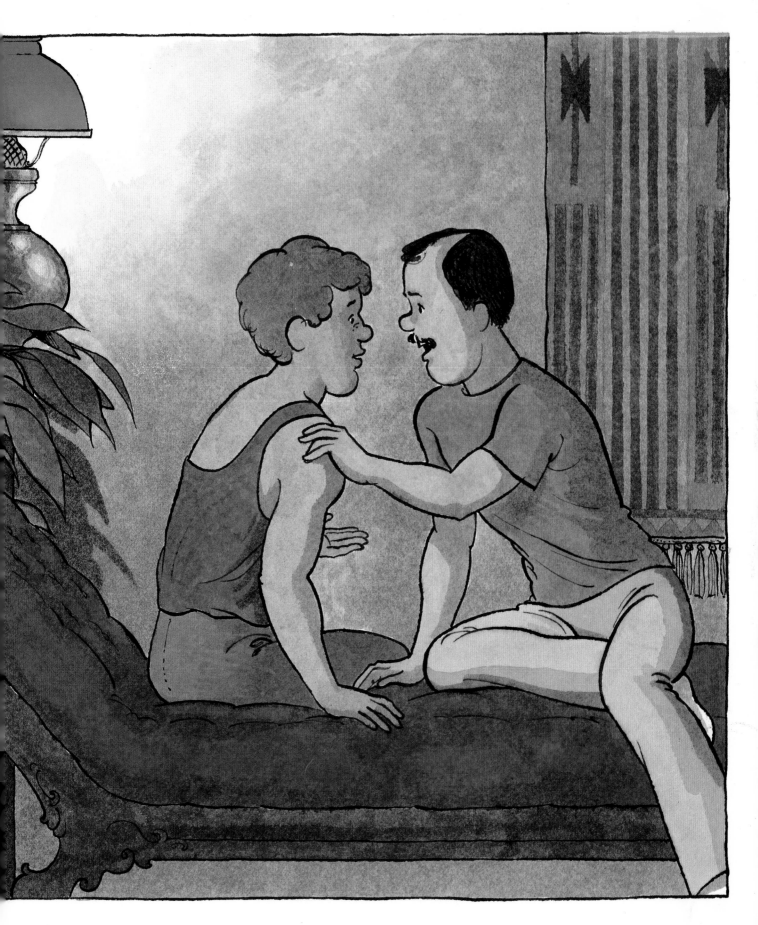

But they always make up.

Frank likes me too!

Just like Daddy, he tells me jokes and riddles,

Helps me catch bugs for show-and-tell,

Reads to me,

Makes *great* peanut butter-and-jelly sandwiches,

And chases nightmares away.

When weekends come,

we do all sorts of things together.

We go to ball games,

Visit the zoo,

Go to the beach,

Work in the yard,

Go shopping,

And in the evenings, we sing at the piano.

Mommy says Daddy and Frank are gay.

At first I didn't know what that meant. So she explained it.

Being gay is just one more kind of love.

And love is the best kind of happiness.

Daddy and his roommate are very happy together,

And I'm happy too!

The author: For years, Michael Willhoite has amused readers of *The Washington Blade* with his cartoons and caricatures. His cartoons have appeared in the book *"Now For My Next Trick..."* and he wrote and illustrated *The 1990 Gay Desk Calendar.*

The Alyson Wonderland series: *Daddy's Roommate* is the first book of this new imprint, which focuses on books for and about the children of lesbian and gay parents. For information about other titles, please write to Alyson Publications, 40 Plympton St., Boston, Mass. 02118, and request an Alyson Wonderland catalog.

ALYSON
WONDERLAND